EMMA'S DRAGON HUNT

STORY & PICTURES BY
CATHERINE STOCK

LOTHROP, LEE & SHEPARD BOOKS · NEW YORK

Copyright © 1984 by Catherine Stock

All rights reserved. No part of this book may be reproduced or utilized in any form or by any means, electronic or mechanical, including photocopying, recording or by any information storage and retrieval system, without permission in writing from the Publisher. Inquiries should be addressed to Lothrop, Lee & Shepard Books, a division of William Morrow & Company, Inc., 105 Madison Avenue, New York, New York 10016.   Printed in the United States of America. First Edition   1 2 3 4 5 6 7 8 9 10

Library of Congress Cataloging in Publication Data

Stock, Catherine.   Emma's dragon hunt.   Summary: Emma's grandfather, newly arrived from China, introduces her to the power of dragons.   [1. Dragons—Fiction.   2. Grandfathers—Fiction]   I. Title. PZ7.S8635Em   1984   [Fic]   83-25109   ISBN 0-688-02696-6   ISBN 0-688-02698-2 (lib. bdg.)

For Ah Yan
and Ah Lee

Special thanks to Barbara

Emma was excited. Her Grandfather Wong
from China was coming to live with them.

But when her grandfather arrived, he didn't look happy.

"The house is right on top of the hill and the roof is too flat," he grumbled. "I can't live here."

Emma looked at her grandfather, puzzled. "Why not, Grandfather?" she asked.

Grandfather Wong turned around and looked at her. "Because there are sure to be dragons living in the hill under the house. They will dance on the flat roof and keep me awake all night," he said.

That night Emma couldn't sleep.

Mother was cross with Grandfather Wong the next morning. "How can Emma concentrate on her lessons when she hasn't slept because of this dragon nonsense?"

"It's not nonsense," Grandfather Wong answered quietly.

That night when Grandfather Wong came in to say good night, Emma had all her stuffed animals with her in bed.

"You mustn't be afraid of the dragons," he said. "Our Chinese dragons are good dragons."

"But what do they look like?" Emma asked nervously.

Grandfather took a deep breath. "A Chinese dragon has the head of a camel, the neck of a snake, the horns of a stag, the eyes of a demon, the ears of a bull, the belly of a clam, the pads of a tiger, the tail of a lizard, the wings and claws of an eagle, the scales of a carp, and the whiskers of Wang Fu, the philosopher."

"Sounds scary to me," whispered Emma.

"No, no. Not at all," Grandfather assured her. "Tomorrow we'll hunt for one. You'll see."

The next morning Emma was so excited that she could hardly wait for Grandfather Wong to finish his second cup of tea.

"Well, now," he said at last. "Dragons like wet and marshy places."

So Emma took Grandfather to see the stream next to the house. She didn't find a dragon, but she did find a ball.

"Dragons love to play ball," said Grandfather Wong. "There must be one close by."

They walked up into the hills. No dragons!
"When it's hot like this, they go underground where it's cooler. These mountains hold many dragon tunnels," explained Grandfather.

Suddenly the earth began to tremble and quake. Emma and her grandfather tumbled down in a heap.

"Was that a dragon?" asked Emma.

Grandfather Wong nodded. "We'll come back tomorrow."

The next day was unusually hot. Emma and Grandfather Wong set off again, hand in hand.

"I made this little paper dragon to put in the sun," he said. "If it gets hot enough, a real dragon sleeping under the hill will wake up."

Everything began to grow dark. Grandfather and Emma looked up at the sky. The sun was slowly disappearing!

"Oh, dear," muttered Grandfather. "The dragon is so angry with the sun for waking him that he is trying to swallow it. But don't worry. The sun is so hot that he'll soon spit it out."

And he did. The sun came out again, but billowy clouds of steam had gathered in the sky. They began to darken. Emma and her grandfather ran for cover as thunder boomed across the sky.

"The dragon is still angry," Grandfather shouted above the noise. "He and his friends are knocking the clouds together. Boom! Boom! Luckily, their sharp claws rip open the clouds and let out all the rain."

It rained and it rained and it rained.

On Monday morning when Emma was getting ready for school, it was still raining.

"I'll ask Shom the Broom's daughter to sweep away those stormy dragons," Grandfather whispered to Emma. "She's a beautiful distant star."

"Where will she sweep them?" asked Emma.

"She sweeps them into the sea with all the clouds," Grandfather told her.

"Oh." Emma looked at a button on her raincoat.

"Dragons hunt for pearls in the sea. Their eyes are so sharp that fishermen paint dragon eyes on their boats to help them find fish," said Grandfather.

"I hope they come back," Emma said softly.

When Emma got home from school, a brisk wind had swept all the clouds away. Her grandfather had a surprise for her, a beautiful dragon kite.

"It's to let the dragons know that we are their friends," he said.

At dinner everyone was talking about the things that had happened since Grandfather had arrived. There had been an earthquake, a heat wave, a solar eclipse, and a terrible thunderstorm followed by a beautiful rainbow.

Grandfather and Emma smiled, but they didn't say anything.

Grandfather Wong let Emma hang the kite in her room that night. She lay in bed and, just as she was falling asleep, she was sure that she could hear the pattering of dancing dragons on the roof.

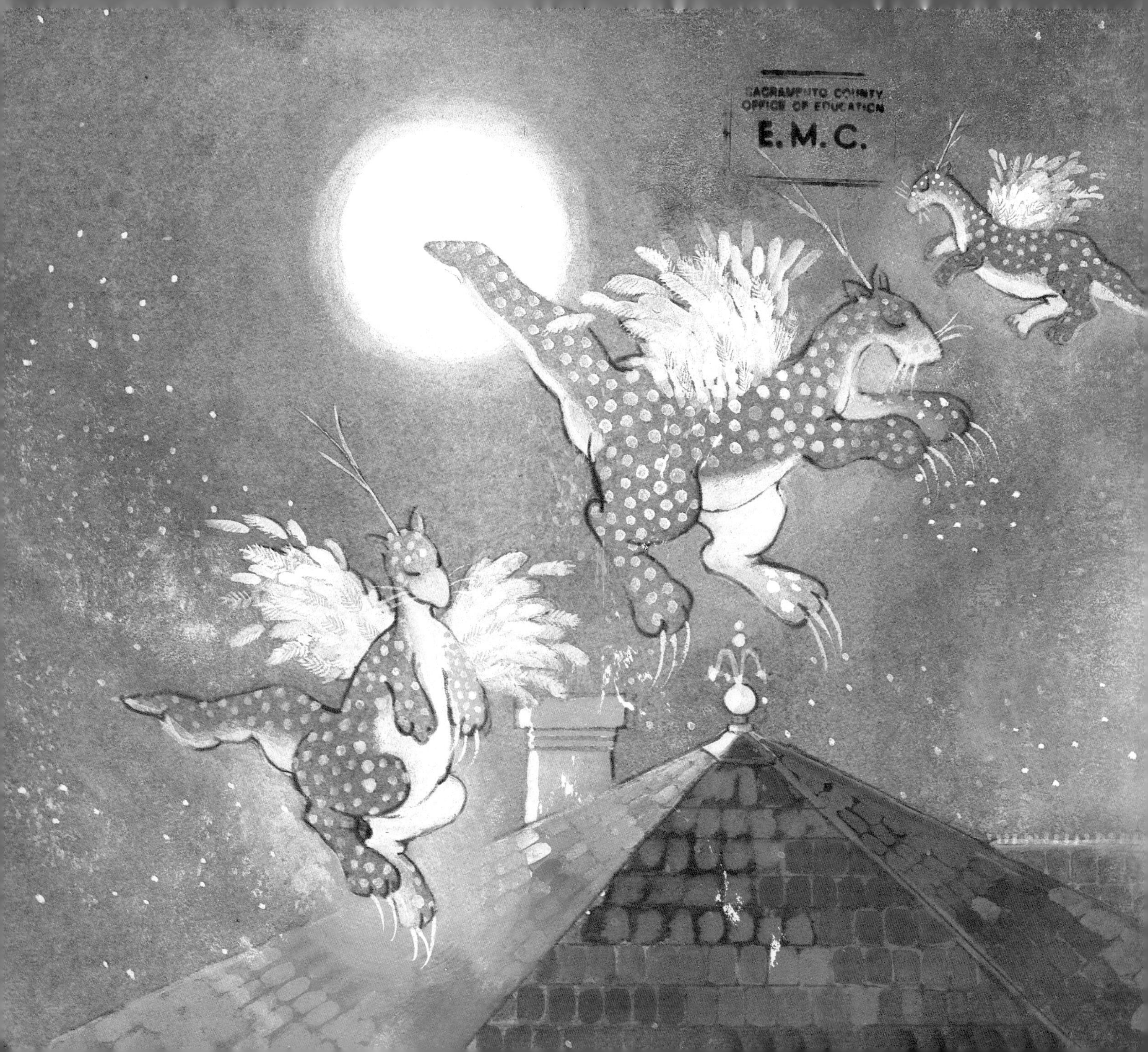